STORIES OF DISCOVERY

INSPIRING BOOKS FOR KIDS 8–12
LEADERSHIP FOR GIRLS

Riley Stone

First Edition

ISBN: 9798873317509

CONTENTS

INTRODUCTION

Dive into a world of inspiring adventures with "Stories of Discovery: Leadership for Girls." This collection of ten stories celebrates the power of imagination, courage, and determination.

Join Sarah as she reaches for the stars, Melody as she finds harmony in diversity, and Sara as she lights up her village with solar-powered dreams.

Witness Luna saving her library, Zara racing for equality, and Ellie unlocking the potential of coding. Be inspired by Bella's creative building, Fiona's sky-high aspirations, Leah's scientific discoveries, and Sarina's journey in finding her voice through writing.

Each tale is a unique journey, teaching that with hard work, creativity, and belief in oneself, anything is possible. Prepare to be captivated and empowered as these stories unfold the magic of dreaming big.

In a small town where every house had a story to tell, there lived a young girl named Sarah. Her room was a galaxy of its own, with glow-in-the-dark stars dotting the ceiling and posters of planets and comets adorning the walls. Each night, Sarah would press her face against the cool glass of her bedroom window, gazing up at the real stars twinkling in the vast sky.

One crisp morning, Sarah bounded into her classroom, her eyes shining with the same brightness as the stars she loved so much. Mr. Jensen, her science teacher, greeted her with a warm smile. "Good morning, Sarah! You seem especially cheerful today."

"Good morning, Mr. Jensen!" Sarah replied, her voice bubbling with excitement. "I saw the Big Dipper last night, clear as day!"

"That's wonderful, Sarah!" Mr. Jensen said. "Your passion for the stars is truly inspiring."

As the day unfolded, Mr. Jensen made an announcement that sent a ripple of excitement through the class. "Next month," he said, "our school will participate in the annual science fair. It's a great opportunity for each of you to explore and present something you're passionate about."

The class buzzed with ideas and chatter, but Sarah sat quietly, her mind racing with possibilities. 'A science project about space,' she thought, 'something that will take everyone on a journey to the stars.'

After class, Sarah approached Mr. Jensen, her eyes sparkling with determination. "Mr. Jensen, I want to create a space project for the science fair. Something that shows the beauty and wonder of the universe."

Mr. Jensen's eyes lit up. "That sounds like a fantastic idea, Sarah. What do you have in mind?"

"I'm not sure yet," Sarah admitted, "but I want it to be something that makes people feel like they're travelling through space, exploring the planets and stars."

"Well, Sarah," Mr. Jensen said, placing a comforting hand on her shoulder, "I believe in you. You have the creativity and drive to make it happen. Remember, the sky's not the limit when it comes to your imagination."

Sarah's heart swelled with encouragement. She spent the rest of the day lost in thoughts of planets and galaxies, her mind weaving together ideas for her project.

That evening, as Sarah sat at her desk, her room bathed in the soft glow of her star-shaped lamp, she began sketching ideas in her notebook. With each stroke of her pencil, her dream project started taking shape, and her journey to the stars began.

As the days passed, Sarah's notebook filled with sketches and ideas for her project. She envisioned a model of the solar system, where each planet could be explored with the touch of a finger. But bringing her vision to life was more challenging than she had imagined.

One afternoon, Sarah and her mother visited the local craft store. Aisle after aisle, Sarah searched for materials that could represent the planets. "Mum, how can I make Saturn's rings? And what about Jupiter's storm?" she asked, her brow furrowed in concentration.

"Let's think creatively," her mother suggested, picking up some glittery paper and foam balls. "These could work for the planets, and maybe this wire for the rings?"

Back home, Sarah set to work. She painted the foam balls in vibrant colors, trying to capture the essence of each planet. But no matter how hard she tried, the rings of Saturn wouldn't stay put, and Jupiter's storm looked more like a blob than a fierce whirlwind.

Feeling frustrated, Sarah took her project to school the next day, hoping Mr. Jensen could offer some advice. "I can't get it right," she sighed, showing him the wobbly rings of Saturn.

Mr. Jensen studied the model thoughtfully. "Remember, Sarah, science is about trial and error. Every great scientist faces challenges. What matters is that you keep trying."

Encouraged by his words, Sarah spent the next few weeks experimenting with different materials and techniques. She stayed up late, her determination unwavering, even when things didn't go as planned.

Then, a new challenge arose. During recess, some of her classmates gathered around her project. "What's this supposed to be?" one of them teased, poking at the foam planets.

"It's my science fair project," Sarah replied, trying to hide her disappointment at their reaction.

"It looks kind of... childish," another classmate laughed before they all walked away.

Sarah's heart sank. Doubt crept into her mind, whispering that maybe her project was too ambitious, too different.

The next day, she shared her concerns with Mr. Jensen. "Maybe they're right," she murmured. "Maybe my project is silly."

Mr. Jensen knelt beside her, his voice earnest. "Sarah, never let anyone dim your shine. Your project is unique, just like you. What's important is that it's your vision, your dream. Keep working on it, and don't be afraid to stand out."

Buoyed by Mr. Jensen's support, Sarah returned to her project with renewed vigor. She worked tirelessly, her imagination taking flight. With each challenge she overcame, her confidence grew, and her model of the solar system began to take on a life of its own.

The science fair was only a week away, and Sarah's solar system model was nearly complete. She had worked hard to perfect each planet, and the once troublesome Saturn now boasted beautiful, stable rings. But just when Sarah thought her challenges were behind her, disaster struck.

While carrying her model to the living room for a final touch-up, Sarah tripped over her little brother's toy car, sending the model crashing to the floor. Planets rolled in every direction, and Saturn's rings snapped in two. Tears welled up in Sarah's eyes as she surveyed the damage. "All my work," she whispered, "ruined."

Hearing the commotion, her mother rushed in. "Oh, Sarah, I'm so sorry," she said, helping her pick up the scattered pieces. "But it's not ruined. We can fix this, together."

The next day, a disheartened Sarah brought the damaged model to school. Mr. Jensen, upon seeing her crestfallen face, asked, "What happened, Sarah?"

"I had an accident," Sarah replied, her voice barely above a whisper. "My project... it's broken."

Mr. Jensen inspected the model carefully. "We can fix this, Sarah. You're not alone in this."

Word of Sarah's mishap spread quickly, and to her surprise, several classmates offered to help. "We can repaint the planets," one said. "And I can help fix Saturn's rings," added another.

Sarah felt a warmth spread through her heart. With the help of her friends and Mr. Jensen, the project was slowly pieced back together. The planets were repainted, Saturn's rings were mended, and the model was stronger than before.

The day of the science fair arrived, and Sarah's project was once again ready. Her hands trembled as she set up her model in the school gym, transformed into a bustling exhibition hall.

As visitors started arriving, Sarah stood nervously by her project. She watched as people passed by, some stopping to admire her work. Her heart pounded in her chest when the judges approached.

"Tell us about your project, Sarah," one judge prompted.

Sarah took a deep breath and began to explain. She talked about each planet, about the challenges she faced, and about the help she received from her friends and Mr. Jensen. As she spoke, her confidence grew, and her passion for the stars shone through.

The judges nodded in appreciation, asking questions and praising her creativity and determination. Sarah answered each query with a newfound confidence, her eyes shining with pride.

As the judges moved on to the next project, Sarah looked around the gym. She saw her classmates presenting their projects, the supportive faces of teachers and parents, and she realized something important. No matter the outcome of the fair, she had already achieved something incredible. She had turned her dream into reality, with resilience and the support of those around her. At that moment, Sarah felt like the brightest star in the sky.

As the science fair drew to a close, excitement buzzed in the air. Sarah watched as the judges huddled together, whispering and nodding. Her heart raced with anticipation. Around her, the gym was a kaleidoscope of projects, each a testament to the creativity and hard work of her classmates.

Finally, the judges took the stage for the awards ceremony. Sarah clasped her hands together, her model of the solar system standing proudly at her booth. "In third place," announced one judge, "a brilliant volcano project!" Applause filled the room as a beaming classmate accepted the award.

"And in second place," the judge continued, "an innovative water purification system!" More applause followed as another student stepped forward.

Sarah's palms were sweaty now. She glanced at Mr. Jensen, who gave her an encouraging smile. 'No matter what happens,' she thought, 'I'm proud of what I've achieved.'

"And now," the head judge said, "the first place in this year's science fair goes to... Sarah, for her outstanding solar system model!"

The gym erupted into cheers. Sarah's mouth fell open in shock, and then, a huge smile spread across her face. She walked up to the stage, her legs feeling like jelly. As she accepted the trophy, she looked out at the crowd, her eyes sparkling.

"Thank you," Sarah said, her voice clear and strong. "This project was a journey, not just through the solar system, but a journey of learning and growing. I couldn't have done it without the support of my friends, my family, and Mr. Jensen. Thank you for believing in me and helping me realize that the sky's not the limit."

Back at her booth, Sarah was surrounded by classmates, congratulating her. "Your project was amazing," one said. "You really deserved to win," another added.

Mr. Jensen approached, his eyes shining with pride. "Sarah, you've done something remarkable today. You turned a dream into reality, and you showed everyone that with hard work and determination, anything is possible."

As Sarah packed up her model, she felt a deep sense of fulfillment. She had faced challenges, but she had persevered. She had doubted herself, but she had overcome. And in the process, she had learned an invaluable lesson: dreaming big and working hard can make even the most ambitious goals achievable.

That night, as Sarah gazed up at the stars, she felt a connection to the universe like never before. The stars seemed to twinkle a little brighter, each one a reminder that in the vastness of space, her journey was just beginning. With a heart full of dreams and a spirit undeterred by obstacles, Sarah knew that her adventure was far from over. For in a universe of endless possibilities, the sky was not the limit.

In the heart of a bustling city, where streets hummed with melodies from around the world, stood a young girl named Melody. Her eyes sparkled with excitement as she gazed at the colorful banners announcing the annual music festival. With her violin case in hand, she danced through the vibrant streets, each step in rhythm with the city's heartbeat.

"Hey, Melody!" called a voice. Melody turned to see Aanya, her friend who could make the tabla talk. Aanya's smile was as bright as the morning sun.

"Are you ready for the festival?" Melody asked, her eyes shining with anticipation.

"Absolutely!" Aanya replied, tapping a rhythm on her tabla case. "But have you heard about the Harmony Challenge?"

Melody's curiosity piqued. "The Harmony Challenge?"

As they walked, they bumped into Carlos, strumming his guitar with fingers that danced like flames. "It's a competition," Carlos explained, his voice as warm as his Latin tunes. "We have to create a piece that blends different musical styles. It's all about harmony in diversity!"

"That sounds amazing!" Melody exclaimed, her mind already swirling with possibilities.

The trio soon reached the festival grounds, where the air buzzed with excitement. There, they met Yara, who played the oud with a touch as gentle as a whisper. Beside her stood Elijah, with his saxophone gleaming like a beacon of jazz.

"Are we thinking what I'm thinking?" Melody asked, her eyes sparkling with an idea.

"Joining the Harmony Challenge?" Elijah guessed, his saxophone glinting in the sunlight.

"Exactly!" Melody beamed. "We can all enter together!"

"But blending our styles will be tough," Yara pointed out, her fingers caressing the strings of her oud.

Hana, who had just joined them with her koto, nodded in agreement. "It's like mixing colors to paint a new picture," she said thoughtfully.

Melody's heart swelled with determination. "But imagine what we could create if we combine our sounds! A symphony of cultures!"

The group huddled together, their excitement building. "We'll need to practice a lot," Carlos said, strumming a chord that seemed to echo their resolve.

"And learn from each other," Aanya added, her hands poised over her tabla.

As they talked, the festival around them burst into life. Music from every corner of the globe filled the air, blending in a beautiful, chaotic harmony that mirrored their own aspirations.

"Let's do it," Melody declared, her violin case clutched tightly. "Let's show the world what happens when different melodies unite!"

With a shared nod, the group of friends set off, their hearts beating in unison with a newfound purpose. The Harmony Challenge wasn't just a competition; it was a journey they were about to embark on, a journey of discovering the beauty in their differences and the magic that could arise when they embraced them together.

The next few days were a whirlwind of music and laughter as Melody and her friends embarked on their musical adventure. They gathered in Melody's backyard, each bringing their own instrument, eager to blend their diverse sounds into one harmonious melody.

"Let's start with something simple," Melody suggested, tuning her violin. "Maybe a melody we all know?"

"How about Twinkle Twinkle Little Star?" Hana proposed, plucking a string on her koto.

"That's perfect!" Carlos agreed, strumming a few chords on his guitar.

They began to play, each instrument weaving its unique sound into the familiar tune. But it wasn't long before they hit a snag. Aanya's tabla rhythm clashed with Elijah's jazz saxophone, and Carlos's guitar struggled to find its place among Yara's oud melodies.

"Wait, stop!" Melody called out, as the music jumbled into discord. "It's not blending right."

"It's like we're all speaking different languages," Yara said, looking puzzled.

"We need to listen to each other more," Elijah suggested. "Let's try again, but this time, let's really focus on what each of us is playing."

They tried once more, paying closer attention to each other's music. Gradually, the notes began to align, creating a unique version of the song that was both familiar and new.

Encouraged by their small success, they decided to explore each other's musical backgrounds. They visited Aanya's home, where her mother taught them about the rhythms of Indian classical music. They listened to Carlos's uncle play flamenco guitar, mesmerized by the rapid, passionate strums. Each visit opened their eyes to the rich histories and emotions behind their friends' music.

However, the more they learned, the more challenges they faced. Trying to incorporate so many different styles into one piece was like fitting puzzle pieces from different sets together.

"We need something that ties our music together," Hana said, a hint of frustration in her voice.

"What if we think about the emotions we want to convey, instead of just the technical parts?" Melody suggested.

They gathered in the city park, where the festival's energy was palpable. Inspired by the sights and sounds around them, they began experimenting with different combinations of their instruments, focusing on the feelings they evoked.

Hours passed as they played, the sun dipping below the horizon, casting a golden glow on their determined faces. They laughed, argued, and occasionally stumbled upon moments of unexpected harmony.

As the night fell, they realized they had created something special. It wasn't perfect, but it was a start—a melody that was more than just a mix of sounds. It was a testament to their friendship and their shared journey.

Exhausted but exhilarated, they packed up their instruments, their spirits lifted by the progress they'd made. The Harmony Challenge was more than a competition; it was a journey that was bringing them closer, not just as musicians, but as friends who shared a love for music and a respect for each other's cultures.
As the day of the Harmony Challenge dawned, the air was thick with anticipation. Melody and her friends gathered early at the festival, instruments in hand, their faces a mix of excitement and nerves.

"We've come so far," Melody said, looking at her friends. "No matter what happens today, I'm proud of us."

"Me too," Elijah agreed, polishing his saxophone. "We've created something really special."

Their turn to perform came all too quickly. The stage loomed large before them, the audience a sea of expectant faces. Taking a deep breath, they stepped into the spotlight, their hearts pounding in unison.

Melody raised her violin, signaling the start. The first notes of their piece floated into the air, a gentle, weaving melody that seemed to whisper of their journey. Aanya's tabla added a rhythmic heartbeat, pulsing with the energy of Indian streets. Carlos's guitar strummed in, bringing a warmth that reminded them of sunny days and dancing feet.

Then Yara's oud sang a song of ancient lands, its mournful beauty intertwining with Hana's koto, which shimmered like a gentle breeze through cherry blossoms. Finally, Elijah's saxophone soared above them all, a soulful cry that spoke of jazz clubs and starlit nights.

The audience was spellbound, caught in the tapestry of sound that Melody and her friends wove together. Their music was more than a blend of different cultures; it was a conversation between friends, each telling their own story, yet listening and responding to the others.

But then, suddenly, a string on Melody's violin snapped. The music faltered, a jarring silence falling over the stage. Melody's heart sank. All their hard work, could it end like this?

Yet, without missing a beat, her friends filled the gap. Aanya's tabla took the lead, its rhythm steady and strong. Carlos, Yara, Hana, and Elijah joined in, their music supporting and lifting each other up, a testament to their unity and strength.

Melody quickly fixed the string, her hands shaking slightly. As she rejoined the piece, her friends welcomed her back with a swell of music, their faces alight with joy and understanding.

Their final notes rang out, a harmonious blend that echoed through the festival grounds, leaving a hush in its wake. Then, as if released from a spell, the audience erupted into applause, their cheers a roaring wave of appreciation and admiration.

The group exchanged glances, their eyes shining with tears of joy. They had done it. They had faced their biggest challenge and emerged stronger, not just as musicians, but as a family bound by the universal language of music.

As they took their bow, the applause washing over them, Melody knew that this moment was about more than winning a competition. It was about the beauty of diversity, the strength found in unity, and the magic that happens when different melodies come together to create a symphony of understanding and friendship.
The cheers from the crowd still echoed in their ears as Melody and her friends stepped off the stage, their hearts light and faces beaming with pride. They had completed their performance, not just flawlessly, but with a passion and unity that had moved everyone who heard it.

As they gathered in a group hug, the festival organizer approached them, a wide smile on his face. "That was incredible!" he exclaimed. "You kids have truly captured the spirit of the Harmony Challenge."

"Did we win?" Carlos asked eagerly, his eyes shining with hope.

The organizer chuckled. "The judges are still deciding, but you've won something much more important. You've won the hearts of everyone here."

The announcement of the results came soon after. The group held hands tightly, waiting in anticipation. "And the winner of the Harmony Challenge is..." the voice boomed over the speakers. A drumroll filled the air.

"Melody and her friends!"

The crowd erupted into applause once again. Melody and her friends looked at each other in disbelief before joy took over, their faces lighting up with exhilarating smiles.

As they walked up to receive their trophy, Melody felt a warmth in her heart. "We did it, together," she whispered to her friends.

Standing before the audience, trophy in hand, Melody addressed the crowd. "This trophy isn't just for us," she said. "It's for every note that brought us closer, every melody that taught us about each other. It's for the music that brought our diverse worlds together in harmony."

The festival ended, but the journey of Melody and her friends was far from over. As they walked home, the streets still echoing with the remnants of music, they talked excitedly about their future plans.

"We should keep playing together," Hana suggested. "We could explore more music, more cultures."

"Yeah," Elijah agreed. "We've started something special. Let's keep it going!"

As they reached Melody's house, they made a pact to continue their musical exploration, to keep learning from each other, and to keep celebrating their diversity.

That night, as Melody lay in bed, she thought about the incredible journey they had embarked on. They had started as individuals, each with their unique style and background. But through music, they had found a common language, a way to connect and understand each other. They had learned that embracing their differences didn't just create beautiful music; it created a bond stronger than any melody.

Melody drifted off to sleep with a smile on her face, the music of her friends' instruments playing like a lullaby in her heart. The Harmony Challenge had taught them all a valuable lesson: that in diversity lies beauty, and in unity lies strength. And when these come together, they create a harmony that resonates far beyond the notes of a song.

In a remote village nestled among rolling hills and whispering forests, where stars twinkled like diamonds in the night sky, lived a girl named Sara. Her world was painted in the hues of nature - emerald greens, earthy browns, and the golden light of lanterns that flickered like fireflies at dusk.

"Sara!" called a voice, warm and familiar. It was her grandfather, a man whose eyes twinkled with knowledge and kindness. "Come, help me with the garden."

As Sara joined her grandfather, the air was filled with the scent of fresh earth and blooming flowers. "Grandpa, why can't we have bright lights like the cities do?" she asked, her curious eyes reflecting the lantern's glow.

Her grandfather smiled, planting a seed gently into the soil. "We live in harmony with nature, Sara. But who knows, maybe one day you'll light up our village in a new way."

Sara pondered this as she worked, her mind always buzzing with questions and ideas. That night, under a blanket of stars, Sara lay thinking about light and darkness, about her village and the vast, unknown world beyond.

The next day at school, Sara's teacher made an exciting announcement. "We're having a science fair," she said, her eyes gleaming with enthusiasm. "The theme is 'Innovations for a Better World'. I encourage all of you to think of ways to make our world a better place."

Sara's heart leapt. Here was her chance to find an answer to the question that twinkled like a star in her mind. She rushed home, bursting with excitement.

"Grandpa, grandpa!" Sara exclaimed, finding her grandfather in his workshop, surrounded by tools and old books. "There's going to be a science fair at school, and I want to create something that will help our village!"

Her grandfather, wiping his hands on his apron, turned to her with a smile. "That's a wonderful idea, Sara. What do you have in mind?"

"I want to find a way to bring light to our village, without harming nature," Sara said, her eyes sparkling with determination.

Her grandfather nodded thoughtfully. "That's a big challenge, but I believe in you. Let's think about this together."

They spent the evening talking about different ideas. Sara's mind was like a sponge, absorbing everything her grandfather said about energy, nature, and inventions.

As the night grew deeper and the lanterns cast a golden glow around them, Sara felt a surge of hope and excitement. She was going to light up her village, not just with lanterns, but with an idea – a bright, shining idea that could change everything.

The next morning, with the sun peeping over the hills, Sara and her grandfather set out on their mission. They started by rummaging through the old tools and materials in the workshop. "What about this, Grandpa?" Sara asked, holding up a tangled mess of wires and metal pieces.

"That's the spirit, Sara!" her grandfather encouraged. "Let's see what we can repurpose."

Their days began to blend into a pattern of trial and error. They experimented with various materials, trying to harness the sun's energy. Sara's grandfather shared stories of his engineering days, which filled Sara with awe and inspiration.

One afternoon, while taking a break under the shade of a large oak tree, Sara noticed the sunlight filtering through the leaves. "Grandpa, look at the light!" she exclaimed. "It's everywhere, but we can't seem to catch it!"

Her grandfather chuckled. "Nature has its ways, Sara. But so do we. Let's keep trying."

As the science fair approached, Sara felt the weight of her challenge. She visited the local library, pouring over books about solar energy. The librarian, Mrs. Hattie, noticed her dedication. "What are you working on, dear?" she asked.

"I'm trying to find a way to bring light to our village using the sun," Sara replied.

"That's quite an ambitious project!" Mrs. Hattie said, impressed. "Here, maybe these books will help."

Sara's eyes lit up with gratitude. Armed with new knowledge, she hurried back to her workshop.

But the journey wasn't smooth. Some villagers doubted her project. "Solar energy in our little village? That's a dreamer's talk," they would say, shaking their heads.

Sara sometimes felt disheartened, but her grandfather's unwavering belief in her kept her going. "Remember, the greatest inventions were once just a dream," he would remind her.

One evening, as they were testing a small solar panel, it flickered to life before quickly fading out. Sara's heart sank. "It's not working, Grandpa," she sighed, her shoulders drooping.

"Don't lose hope, Sara," her grandfather said gently. "Every failure is a step closer to success."

Days turned into nights, and nights into days, as Sara and her grandfather continued their experiments. They faced setbacks - broken components, uncooperative weather, and moments of doubt. But Sara's determination never wavered.

As the day of the science fair dawned, Sara looked at their creation – a humble, yet hopeful prototype of a solar-powered light. It wasn't perfect, but it was a start – a spark that could ignite a brighter future for her village. With her grandfather's encouraging smile, Sara prepared to share her dream with the world, ready to face whatever came next.

On the morning of the science fair, Sara and her grandfather arrived at the school with their prototype. Sara's hands trembled slightly as she set up her project, a modest solar panel connected to a small, handcrafted light.

As students and teachers gathered around, Sara began to explain her project. "This is a solar-powered light. It's a way to bring sustainable light to our village using the sun's energy," she said, her voice steady and clear.

The crowd listened intently, their faces a mix of curiosity and skepticism. Sara demonstrated how the solar panel absorbed sunlight and converted it into electricity, lighting up the small bulb.

Just then, a cloud passed overhead, casting a shadow over the solar panel. The light flickered and went out, causing a murmur to ripple through the crowd.

Sara's heart sank. She looked at her grandfather, who gave her a reassuring nod. "Remember, Sara, it's not about perfection. It's about the effort and the idea," he whispered.

Sara took a deep breath and addressed the crowd. "This is part of the challenge. Our village is often cloudy, but that doesn't mean we can't use solar energy. We just need to think creatively and persistently," she said, her voice growing stronger.

As she spoke, the cloud moved away, and sunlight bathed the solar panel once more. The light flickered back to life, brighter than before. A gasp went through the crowd, followed by applause.

Sara's teacher, Ms. Jenkins, stepped forward, her eyes shining with pride. "Sara, you've shown us that with determination and innovation, we can find solutions to our challenges. You've truly embodied the spirit of this science fair."

The other students crowded around, asking questions and marveling at the simple yet effective technology. Sara answered each question with confidence, explaining the potential of solar energy and her plans to improve the design.

As the fair came to a close, the judges announced the winners. Sara's name was called for the 'Most Innovative Project' award. Her heart swelled with joy and pride as she accepted the award, her grandfather beaming beside her.

That evening, as they walked back to their village, her grandfather said, "You've lit up more than just a bulb today, Sara. You've lit up the minds and hearts of our people."

Sara looked up at the stars, twinkling like countless tiny lights in the sky. She felt a deep sense of accomplishment and hope. She had taken the first step towards her dream, lighting up her village not just with light, but with the promise of a brighter future.

Back in the village, news of Sara's success at the science fair spread like wildfire. Villagers, young and old, gathered around her, eager to hear about her invention. Sara, with newfound confidence, explained how the solar-powered light worked and how it could benefit the village.

Her grandfather watched with pride as Sara spoke. "I always knew you could do it," he whispered to her. "You've brought a new light to our village, in more ways than one."

The village chief, Mr. Johansson, approached Sara. "Your project has opened our eyes, Sara. We've been hesitant about new ideas, but you've shown us the way forward. What do you need to make this a reality for our village?"

Sara's eyes gleamed with excitement. "We need to build more solar panels and lights. It will take time and effort, but together, we can light up every home in our village."

The villagers nodded in agreement, their faces alight with enthusiasm. They offered their help - carpenters, electricians, and even the children wanted to be a part of this change.

Over the next few weeks, the village transformed. Sara and her grandfather led teams of villagers, building and installing solar panels on rooftops. There were challenges, of course - days when the sun didn't shine, or when a panel didn't work as expected. But Sara's resilience inspired everyone to keep trying, to keep improving.

Finally, the night arrived when they were ready to test the lights. As the sun set, the villagers gathered in the central square, holding their breath. Sara, with a small remote in her hand, pressed a button.

One by one, the lights flickered on, bathing the village in a soft, warm glow. Gasps and cheers erupted from the crowd. Children danced around, their laughter mingling with the chatter of the adults.

"This is incredible, Sara," Mr. Johansson said, his voice filled with emotion. "You've not only brought us light but also hope and unity."

Sara looked around at the smiling faces of her fellow villagers, their homes aglow in the gentle light. She felt a surge of joy and pride. "We did this together," she said. "We can achieve great things when we believe in ourselves and work together."

That night, as Sara lay in bed, she thought about the journey she had undertaken. She had turned a dream into reality, not just for herself, but for her entire village. She had learned that with determination, creativity, and collaboration, even the toughest challenges could be overcome.

And as she drifted off to sleep, the village outside her window shimmered in the gentle light of their collective achievement, a testament to the power of dreams and the spirit of innovation.

In a small town where every street was lined with blossoming trees and cheerful houses, there stood a library unlike any other. Its walls were painted with murals of faraway lands and mythical creatures, and its windows always glowed warmly, inviting everyone inside.

Luna, with her bright eyes full of wonder, pushed open the heavy wooden door of the library. The familiar smell of old books and the soft hum of hushed conversations wrapped around her like a cozy blanket. She skipped past rows of bookshelves, each filled with stories waiting to be discovered.

"Good afternoon, Luna," greeted Mrs. Flores, the librarian, from behind her large, cluttered desk. Mrs. Flores had kind eyes and a gentle smile that made everyone feel at home.

"Hi, Mrs. Flores!" Luna beamed, placing a stack of books on the counter. "I've read all these! Do you have any new adventure stories?"

Mrs. Flores chuckled, her eyes twinkling. "For you, Luna, there's always something new." She rummaged through a pile of books, finally pulling out a bright, illustrated cover. "How about this one? It's about a pirate queen and her magical compass."

Luna's eyes sparkled. "That sounds amazing! Thank you, Mrs. Flores."

As Luna tucked the book under her arm, the bell above the library door jingled. Mr. Perkins, the town mayor, stepped in, his face unusually serious.

"Mrs. Flores, can I have a word?" he asked, glancing around the library.

"Of course, Mr. Perkins. Luna, why don't you start on your new book? I'll be right back."

Luna found her favorite spot, a cozy corner with a plush armchair, and delved into the world of the pirate queen. But her attention was soon drawn to the low, urgent conversation between Mrs. Flores and Mr. Perkins.

"We simply don't have the funds to keep the library running," she overheard Mr. Perkins say. "I'm afraid we'll have to close it down."

Close the library? Luna's heart sank. This place was her sanctuary, a gateway to countless adventures and dreams. It couldn't just disappear.

"But the library is the heart of our town," Mrs. Flores protested. "You can't take that away from the children, from everyone."

"I'm truly sorry, but my hands are tied," Mr. Perkins replied, sounding genuinely regretful.

As they continued to talk, Luna sat frozen, the book lying forgotten in her lap. The thought of losing the library was unthinkable. She knew she had to do something. But what?

Determined, Luna stood up, her mind racing with ideas. The library was more than just a building with books; it was a treasure chest of knowledge and imagination, and she was going to fight to keep it open.

Luna approached Mrs. Flores, determination etched on her face. "We can't let them close the library. We have to do something."

Mrs. Flores sighed, a sad smile crossing her face. "I wish it were that simple, Luna. But the town council has made up its mind."

"But we can't just give up!" Luna's voice trembled with passion. "This library means everything to me, to all of us. There has to be a way to save it."

Seeing the fire in Luna's eyes, Mrs. Flores nodded slowly. "Alright, let's think this through. What if we show the town council how much the library means to everyone?"

Luna's eyes lit up. "Yes! We can organize a town meeting. Everyone can share their stories about the library."

With a plan in mind, Luna dashed out of the library, her mind buzzing with excitement. She spoke to her friends, her teacher, the baker, and even the postman, telling them about the meeting and urging them to come.

Word spread quickly, and soon the whole town was abuzz with talk of saving the library. Luna spent her afternoons creating posters and handing out flyers, her enthusiasm contagious.

The day of the meeting arrived. The library was packed with people of all ages, their faces a mix of concern and hope. Luna stood at the front, her heart pounding.

"Thank you, everyone, for coming," she began, her voice steady. "This library isn't just a building; it's a place where we learn, dream, and grow. We can't let it close."

One by one, people stood up to speak. An elderly man talked about how the library had been his haven after his wife passed away. A young mother shared how the children's reading hour had helped her daughter overcome her shyness. Even Mr. Jenkins, the gruff mechanic, admitted how the DIY books had saved him money on car repairs.

The stories were heartfelt and powerful, painting a picture of a library that was much more than just a collection of books. It was a cornerstone of the community, a place where memories were made, and lives were changed.

As the meeting drew to a close, Luna felt a surge of hope. "Let's take these stories to the town council," she urged. "Let's show them that the library is worth fighting for."

The crowd erupted in applause, their faces alight with determination. They were ready to stand up for their beloved library, inspired by the courage and passion of a young girl who believed in the power of knowledge and community.

Luna smiled, her heart full. Together, they could make a difference. The fight to save the library had just begun.

Luna, Mrs. Flores, and a group of dedicated townsfolk stood outside the town hall, their hands clutching homemade signs that read 'Save Our Library'. Inside, the town council was about to meet, and this was their chance to make a stand.

Mrs. Flores squeezed Luna's hand. "Are you ready?" she asked.

Luna nodded, feeling a mix of nerves and excitement. "Let's do this."

The meeting room was filled with council members, looking surprised at the unexpected audience. Luna stepped forward, her voice clear and strong. "We're here to talk about the library. It's more than just a building. It's a part of our lives."

The council members exchanged glances, some looking uneasy, others indifferent. The mayor, Mr. Perkins, gave a slight nod, signaling Luna to continue.

Luna talked about the meeting they had held, sharing the stories and sentiments of the town's residents. Mrs. Flores added her perspective, speaking about the library's role in education and community building.

As they spoke, a hush fell over the room. The council members listened, some visibly moved by the heartfelt pleas. But then, the head of the council, Mr. Davidson, spoke up. "While your stories are touching, the fact remains that the library is a financial burden we can no longer shoulder."

The room fell silent, the air heavy with disappointment. Luna's heart sank, but just then, Mrs. Flores stepped forward with a determined look. "May I say one more thing?" she asked. The council nodded.

Mrs. Flores pulled out an old, dusty book and opened it to a marked page. "This is a record of the town's history. It states that when the library was built, a decree was made, ensuring it would always remain open as a community educational resource."

The room buzzed with murmurs as Mrs. Flores read the decree aloud. Mr. Davidson looked taken aback, flipping through his papers. "We... we weren't aware of this," he stammered.

Luna watched, her heart pounding, as the council members conferred in hushed tones. After what felt like an eternity, Mr. Perkins stood up. "In light of this new information, we need to reconsider our decision. The library will remain open while we explore alternative funding solutions."

A wave of relief and joy swept through the room. Luna beamed, her eyes shining with tears of happiness. They had done it. They had saved the library.

The townsfolk erupted into cheers and applause, hugging each other and smiling broadly. Luna looked around at the jubilant faces, feeling a deep sense of pride and accomplishment. Together, they had shown that their voices mattered, that they could make a difference.

As the crowd began to disperse, Luna turned to Mrs. Flores, her smile wide and grateful. "We did it, Mrs. Flores. We saved the library."

Mrs. Flores hugged Luna tightly. "Yes, we did. And it's all thanks to you, Luna. You've shown us all the true power of standing up for what you believe in."

The following days in the small town were filled with a newfound energy and joy. News of the library's salvation spread like wildfire, igniting smiles and conversations everywhere.

Luna walked into the library, now buzzing with more visitors than ever. The walls echoed with laughter and chatter, a stark contrast to the silence that had threatened to engulf it just weeks before.

Mrs. Flores, standing amidst a group of children gathered for story time, caught Luna's eye and beamed at her. "Luna, come over here," she called.

Luna made her way through the crowd, her heart swelling with pride at the sight of the thriving library. "I have someone I'd like you to meet," Mrs. Flores said, gesturing to a lady standing next to her.

"This is Ms. Bennett from the town council," Mrs. Flores introduced. "She has some news for you."

Ms. Bennett smiled warmly at Luna. "Hello, Luna. I wanted to thank you personally for what you've done. Your passion and determination have inspired the council. We've found a way to secure funding for the library, and we're planning to expand the children's section."

Luna's eyes widened in surprise and delight. "Really? That's amazing!"

"Yes," Ms. Bennett continued. "And we would like you to be a part of the planning committee, as a representative of the town's young readers."

Luna couldn't believe her ears. She was going to help shape the future of her beloved library. "I'd love to!" she exclaimed.

The room erupted into applause once again, and Luna felt a warmth spread through her chest. She had not only saved her favorite place but was now going to be a part of its growth.

As the crowd dispersed, Luna turned to Mrs. Flores. "I can't believe this is all happening because of us."

Mrs. Flores smiled, placing a hand on Luna's shoulder. "No, Luna. It happened because of you. You showed us that one person, no matter how small, can make a big difference."

Luna looked around at the happy faces in the library, her heart full. She had learned something valuable: that her voice mattered, that she could change the world around her.

The library had always been a place of magic and wonder for Luna, but now it held a new meaning. It was a symbol of her courage, a testament to the power of standing up for what you believe in.

As Luna left the library that day, the sun setting in a blaze of colors, she knew this was just the beginning of many more adventures and battles she would fight, armed with knowledge and a fearless heart.

Zara tightened the last bolt on her go-kart, her hands deftly spinning the wrench. The sun cast a warm glow over the bustling go-kart racing track, alive with the sounds of engines and laughter. Today was not just any day at the track; it was the beginning of something special.

"Looking good, Zara!" called Coach Patel, walking over with a proud smile. "Ready for the big announcement?"

Zara nodded, wiping her hands on her overalls. "I can't wait, Coach. Whatever it is, I'm ready for it."

As they walked towards the announcement area, Zara's friends from her racing team joined them. There was Ali, always quick with a joke, and Mia, whose knowledge of karts was unmatched. They were a team, united by their love for racing and their belief in each other.

The track owner, Mr. Thompson, stood on a small podium, his voice booming through the speakers. "Welcome, racers and families! This year, we're making history. Our junior championship will be a mixed-gender event for the first time!"

Whispers and murmurs rippled through the crowd. Zara's heart raced with excitement. A mixed-gender race meant competing against everyone, and she knew she had what it took.

"That's amazing!" exclaimed Mia. "It's about time everyone got to race together."

"Yeah," Ali added, "Zara's going to show them how it's done!"

But not everyone seemed thrilled. A few racers huddled together, casting doubtful glances in Zara's direction.

"Think a girl can really compete against us?" one of them snickered.

Zara heard them but didn't waver. She knew her skill and determination spoke louder than their doubts.

Coach Patel put a hand on her shoulder. "Don't mind them, Zara. You've got this. Remember, it's your skill that counts, not their opinions."

Zara nodded, her resolve firm. "I'm here to race, Coach. And I'm here to win."

The sun began to set, casting long shadows over the track. Zara looked around at her team, her friends, and the track she loved. This was her world, and she was ready to show it what she could do.

As the day came to an end, Zara and her team headed home, their minds buzzing with excitement and anticipation. The race was a week away, but for Zara, it was more than just a competition. It was a chance to prove that on the track, everyone was equal, and anything was possible.

The days leading up to the race were a whirlwind of activity. Each morning, as the sun peeked over the horizon, Zara was already at the track, her go-kart roaring to life. She practiced her turns, perfected her starts, and pushed her kart to its limits. Mia and Ali were always there, offering tips and encouragement.

"Try taking the corner a bit wider," Mia suggested during one practice session, watching intently as Zara navigated the track.

"That's it! You're getting faster every day," cheered Ali, his eyes following Zara's kart as it zoomed past.

But it wasn't all smooth driving. The skepticism from some of the other racers continued to grow. They whispered as she passed, their words sharp and doubting.

"Does she really think she can keep up with us?" one of them muttered loud enough for Zara to hear.

Zara felt a sting of annoyance, but she didn't let it slow her down. She knew her worth, and she wasn't going to let anyone's doubts define her.

The day before the race, the track hosted a meet-and-greet for all the competitors. Zara and her team arrived, greeted by the excited chatter of racers and the smell of fresh popcorn from the concession stands.

As Zara walked through the crowd, she overheard more comments. "She's good, but racing against the boys? That's a different story."

Zara's grip tightened on her racing helmet. She glanced at Coach Patel, who gave her an encouraging nod. It was all the reassurance she needed.

The meet-and-greet ended with a speech from Mr. Thompson. "Tomorrow, you'll all make history. Remember, this race is about sportsmanship and proving that talent knows no gender. Good luck to all!"

That night, Zara lay in bed, her mind racing faster than her kart. She thought about the track, the turns she had mastered, and the skeptics she would prove wrong. She was ready.

The morning of the race dawned bright and clear. The air was electric with anticipation as racers and spectators gathered at the track.

Zara, dressed in her racing suit, felt a surge of excitement. Her kart, polished and ready, gleamed in the morning sun.

"You've got this, Zara," said Mia, giving her a thumbs-up.

"We believe in you," added Ali, his smile wide and supportive.

Zara climbed into her kart, feeling the familiar thrill of the driver's seat. She looked around at her competitors, their faces focused and determined.

The starting lights began to count down. Red... yellow... green!

The karts roared to life, and they were off! Zara's kart surged forward, the wind whipping past her helmet as she accelerated down the track.

The race was on, and Zara was in her element, her heart pounding with the thrill of the chase. She was not just racing for herself; she was racing for every girl who had ever been told they couldn't. And she was determined to win.

The race was intense, with each kart jostling for position. Zara's focus was unwavering as she navigated the track, her kart hugging the curves tightly. She could hear the roar of the engines and the cheers of the crowd, but it all faded into the background as she concentrated on the track ahead.

"Keep it up, Zara! You're doing great!" shouted Coach Patel from the sidelines, his voice barely audible over the noise.

Zara was in fourth place, but she was gaining on the kart in front of her. She eyed the next turn, a sharp one that she had practiced many times. This was her chance.

As she approached the turn, she took a deep breath and steered sharply, her kart sliding just a bit but holding on. She passed the third-place kart, a cheer erupting from her team.

But the race was far from over. The two lead karts were ahead, and they were fast. Zara pushed her kart, feeling the engine strain under her demand for more speed.

Up ahead, the two leading karts were neck and neck. Zara watched as they took a turn too sharply, bumping into each other. One kart wobbled, losing momentum. Zara seized the opportunity, zooming past into second place.

Now it was just her and the leading kart. The driver, a boy with a reputation for being the fastest, glanced back at her. Zara could see the surprise in his eyes. She was not just a competitor; she was a threat.

The final lap began, and the tension was palpable. Zara's kart was close behind the leader, waiting for the right moment.

As they approached the final turn, the leading kart made a small mistake, swerving slightly. Zara knew this was her moment. She steered her kart with precision, edging closer.

"Go, Zara, go!" her team yelled, jumping up and down in excitement.

Side by side, they approached the finish line. Zara pushed her kart to its limits, her heart pounding in her chest.

And then, in a burst of speed, she pulled ahead, crossing the finish line first. The crowd erupted into cheers and applause.

Zara slowed her kart to a stop, her breath coming in quick gasps. She had done it. She had won!

Her team rushed onto the track, lifting her into the air. "You did it, Zara! You showed them all!"

Zara's eyes were bright with tears of joy. She had overcome the doubts, the whispers, and the skepticism. She had proven that skill and determination were what mattered, not gender.

As she stood there, surrounded by her cheering team, Zara knew this was a moment she would never forget. She had raced for equality, and she had emerged victorious.

As Zara stood on the podium, the gold medal gleaming around her neck, the cheers of the crowd filled the air. She looked out at the sea of faces, her heart swelling with pride and joy. She had done more than win a race; she had broken barriers and challenged stereotypes.

Mr. Thompson stepped forward, microphone in hand. "Ladies and gentlemen, let's hear it for Zara, our champion, who has shown us that talent and determination know no gender!"

The applause was deafening. Zara's eyes scanned the crowd, landing on her team, who were beaming with pride. Coach Patel wiped a tear from his eye, his usual composure replaced by unabashed joy.

As the ceremony concluded, the other racers approached Zara. The boy who had finished second extended his hand. "That was some incredible racing, Zara. You were amazing out there."

"Thanks," Zara replied, shaking his hand. "It was a great race."

"You've changed my mind," another racer admitted. "I didn't think a girl could race like that. I was wrong."

Zara smiled, her heart light. "We all have the same track, the same karts. It's how we race that makes the difference."

The sun was setting, casting a warm, golden hue over the track. Zara and her team gathered their gear, still buzzing with the excitement of the day.

"Zara, you were like a lightning bolt out there!" exclaimed Mia.

"Yeah, you showed everyone what you're made of," added Ali.

As they walked away from the track, Zara felt a deep sense of fulfillment. She had not only achieved her own dream but had also opened the minds of others.

"You know, Zara," said Coach Patel, "you've done more than win a race today. You've shown that it's not about being a boy or a girl. It's about being a racer, being a person who strives and succeeds."

Zara nodded, her eyes reflecting the last rays of the setting sun. "I just wanted to race, Coach. To do what I love. But if I've helped change how people see things, then that's even better."

They reached the car, and Zara took one last look at the track, her heart full of memories and triumphs. She knew this was just the beginning of her journey, a journey not just about racing, but about proving that anyone could achieve their dreams, regardless of who they were.

As they drove off, Zara felt a sense of peace. She had raced for equality, for the right to be seen as a racer, not just a girl. And in that race, she had zoomed ahead, not just on the track, but in the hearts and minds of all who watched.

Ellie peered through the glass window of the tech club room, her eyes wide with a mix of curiosity and hesitation. Inside, students clustered around glowing computer screens, their fingers dancing across keyboards as colorful code filled the monitors. The buzz of excited chatter and the occasional cheer filled the air, creating an atmosphere of vibrant creativity.

Taking a deep breath, Ellie pushed the door open and stepped inside. The room, lined with posters of robots and famous inventors, felt like stepping into a future world. At the front, Mr. Lee, the computer teacher, was setting up a projector, his face lighting up with a welcoming smile as he noticed Ellie.

"Ah, Ellie! So glad you could join us," Mr. Lee said, his voice warm and encouraging. "Welcome to the tech club. Here, we learn, create, and most importantly, have fun with technology."

Ellie nodded, her heart fluttering with excitement and nervousness. She had always been fascinated by computers and gadgets, but the thought of actually creating something with technology seemed daunting.

As she found a seat, a boy next to her grinned. "First time at the club?" he asked.

"Yeah," Ellie replied, trying to sound confident. "I've never done coding or anything like that before."

"Don't worry, you'll love it. Mr. Lee makes everything super interesting," the boy reassured her.

Mr. Lee clapped his hands, drawing everyone's attention. "Alright, everyone, let's get started. Today, we're going to discuss our upcoming project for the school-wide coding competition. It's a chance for you all to show off your skills and maybe even get to present your project at the local tech fair!"

The room buzzed with excitement. A coding competition? The thought both thrilled and terrified Ellie.

"We'll be working in teams or individually to create something unique," Mr. Lee continued. "It could be a game, an app, a robot – anything, as long as it involves coding."

Ellie's mind raced with ideas. A game... maybe she could create a game. But the doubt crept in. Could she really do it?

As if reading her thoughts, Mr. Lee added, "Remember, it's not just about winning. It's about learning new skills, solving problems, and most importantly, having fun. I'm here to help you every step of the way."

Ellie felt a spark of determination. Maybe, just maybe, she could do this. With Mr. Lee's help and her own creativity, she could turn her fascination with technology into something real. This was her chance to dive into the world of coding, and she was ready to take the leap.

As the days passed, Ellie found herself immersed in the world of coding. Each afternoon, she hurried to the tech club, eager to learn and experiment. Mr. Lee introduced the basics of coding, and Ellie absorbed every word, every instruction, as if it were a secret language only she could understand.

"Think of coding like giving instructions to a computer," Mr. Lee explained one day. "You're the boss, telling it exactly what to do."

Ellie loved that idea – being in control, creating something from nothing but lines of code. She decided to work on her own project for the competition – a game that combined storytelling with puzzles. It was ambitious, especially for a beginner, but she felt driven by a force she couldn't explain.

Her game, "Mystery of the Enchanted Forest," was set in a magical world. Players would solve puzzles to unlock secrets and progress through the story. Ellie spent hours sketching ideas, plotting the storyline, and thinking about the puzzles.

However, with ambition came challenges. Coding was like solving a puzzle, but sometimes the pieces didn't fit. Ellie often found herself staring at her screen, trying to figure out why her code wasn't working.

"Everything okay, Ellie?" Mr. Lee would ask during these moments.

"Yeah, just trying to figure out this bug," Ellie would respond, her forehead creased in concentration.

"Don't give up. Break the problem down, and you'll find the solution," Mr. Lee would encourage, his words a gentle push towards perseverance.

As the competition neared, the club's atmosphere grew more intense. Some students worked in teams, their voices a mix of debate and laughter. Others, like Ellie, preferred the quiet focus of solo work, their expressions a reflection of internal thought processes.

Ellie's game was taking shape, but it was far from complete. She often stayed late, her fingers flying over the keyboard as she added new features or fixed bugs. The story of her enchanted forest was coming to life, and with each line of code, Ellie felt more connected to her creation.

One day, a group of students gathered around Ellie's computer. "Wow, that looks cool!" one of them exclaimed, pointing at the screen where a beautifully designed forest landscape awaited the player's exploration.

"Thanks," Ellie beamed, a swell of pride rising in her chest. "It's for the competition."

"You did this all by yourself?" another student asked, impressed.

"Yeah, it's been tough, but I'm learning a lot," Ellie replied, her confidence growing with each word.

Her project was more than just a game; it was a testament to her hard work, creativity, and newfound love for coding. With each challenge she overcame, Ellie felt more empowered, more capable. The competition was no longer just a contest; it was a journey of discovery, and Ellie was determined to see it through.

The day before the competition, Ellie faced her biggest challenge yet. A critical bug in her game caused it to crash every time a player tried to enter the enchanted forest. Frantically, she scoured her code, searching for the error. The lines of text seemed to blur before her eyes, each *if* and *else* merging into an indecipherable jumble.

She felt a tap on her shoulder. It was Mr. Lee. "Ellie, you've been at this for hours. Maybe take a break?"

Ellie shook her head, her eyes fixed on the screen. "I can't, Mr. Lee. The competition is tomorrow, and my game keeps crashing. I don't know what to do."

Mr. Lee pulled up a chair beside her. "Let's look at it together. Sometimes, a fresh pair of eyes can spot what you've missed."

Together, they combed through the code, Ellie explaining her logic and Mr. Lee offering suggestions. Time seemed to stand still as they worked, the only sounds in the room were the click of the mouse and the hum of the computer.

"Here," Mr. Lee finally said, pointing to a section of code. "This loop is causing the crash. You need to close it properly."

Ellie's eyes widened as she spotted the mistake. A wave of relief washed over her. With trembling fingers, she corrected the code and ran the game. It worked flawlessly, the enchanted forest springing to life on the screen.

"I did it!" Ellie exclaimed, a broad smile spreading across her face.

"You did," Mr. Lee agreed, smiling back. "See, you had the solution all along. You just needed a little nudge in the right direction."

That night, Ellie lay in bed, her mind replaying the day's events. She had overcome so many obstacles, learned so much. No matter what happened at the competition, she was proud of herself and what she had accomplished.

The next morning, Ellie arrived at the competition, her game saved on a USB drive. Her heart raced with a mix of nerves and excitement as she set up her project in the designated area.

Students from other schools had also brought their projects, and Ellie couldn't help but feel awed by their creativity. Robots, apps, and games filled the room, each a testament to the skill and imagination of its creator.

Finally, it was Ellie's turn to present. She stood before the judges, her game projected onto a large screen. As she explained the concept, the challenges she faced, and how she overcame them, she felt a sense of confidence she had never known before.

She ended her presentation with a live demonstration of "Mystery of the Enchanted Forest." The game ran smoothly, its puzzles engaging and its story captivating. The judges nodded appreciatively, their faces showing genuine interest.

As Ellie stepped down, she felt a surge of triumph. She had not only created a game but had also embarked on a journey of self-discovery and growth. No matter the outcome, she knew she had achieved something remarkable.

As the judges deliberated, a buzz of anticipation filled the room. Ellie, standing by her project, felt a sense of calm. She had done her best, and that was what mattered most.

Finally, the judges returned, their expressions inscrutable. "We've seen incredible talent today," one judge began, "and choosing the winners was no easy task."

Ellie held her breath as the judges announced the third and second place winners. Then came the moment of truth. "And the first place goes to... Ellie, for her game 'Mystery of the Enchanted Forest!'"

The room erupted in applause. Ellie's heart leapt. She had won! Walking up to receive her award, she felt a mixture of disbelief and pride.

"Your game showed not only technical skill but also creativity and storytelling," the judge said, handing her the trophy. "It's clear you put your heart and soul into this project."

Back at school the next day, Mr. Lee congratulated Ellie in front of the whole tech club. "Ellie's success is a testament to her hard work and determination. She's an inspiration to us all."

Ellie beamed, feeling her cheeks flush with pride. "Thank you, Mr. Lee. I couldn't have done it without your guidance and support."

As her classmates clapped, Ellie realized the true extent of her journey. She had started as a curious but unsure girl, and now she was a confident coder, a creator of worlds.

Later, as Ellie sat before her computer, starting a new project, she reflected on her experience. The coding competition had been about more than just winning. It was about facing challenges, learning from mistakes, and pushing beyond her limits.

She had learned that with perseverance and a willingness to learn, she could overcome any obstacle. Coding had opened a door to a world of possibilities, and Ellie was eager to explore them all.

And so, "The Code of Courage: Ellie's Tech Triumph" came to an end, not with a final full stop, but with an ellipsis, a promise of more adventures and creations to come.

Through Ellie's journey, the story conveyed a powerful moral: Learning new skills, like coding, can unlock unexpected doors and opportunities. It taught that courage, curiosity, and perseverance are the keys to overcoming challenges and achieving one's dreams. Ellie's story was a testament to the boundless potential within every child, a reminder that with dedication and hard work, anything is possible.

In the heart of a bustling town, where laughter and music danced through the air, stood a vibrant community center, its walls adorned with colorful murals that told stories of joy and creativity. It was a special place for Bella, a girl with a vivid imagination and a love for building dreams out of tiny blocks.

On a sunny Saturday morning, Bella sat cross-legged on her bedroom floor, surrounded by sketches of castles, towers, and fantastical creatures, all born from her boundless imagination. Her fingers danced over the colorful blocks scattered around her, each one a building block of her grand visions.

"Building again, Bella?" her mother asked, peeking into the room with a warm smile.

"Yes, Mum! Look at this!" Bella held up a sketch of a towering structure, her eyes sparkling with excitement. "I'm going to make it real one day."

As Bella continued to build, her little world was interrupted by a knock on the door. It was Max, her best friend, with a grin as wide as the Thames.

"Hey, Bella! Did you hear about the contest at the community center? A building block contest!" Max exclaimed, barely able to contain his excitement.

Bella's eyes widened. "Really? That sounds amazing!"

"They're inviting all kids to create something unique. I thought of you immediately!" Max said, sitting down beside her.

Bella bit her lip, a mixture of excitement and nervousness swirling inside her. "But, what if my ideas aren't good enough?"

Max looked around at her sketches and the structures she had already built. "Are you kidding? Your ideas are brilliant! You have to show them off."

Encouraged by Max's words, Bella's confidence began to bloom. "Alright, let's do it! We'll make the most amazing structure they've ever seen!"

The next few days were a whirlwind of planning and preparation. Bella and Max spent hours discussing ideas, combining Bella's creative flair with Max's practical insights. Together, they sketched a design that was both ambitious and awe-inspiring.

On the day of the contest, the community center was abuzz with excitement. Children of all ages were there, their tables overflowing with blocks of every shape and color. The air was filled with the sounds of laughter and the clinking of blocks being stacked and arranged.

Bella and Max found their spot, a small table near the window where sunlight poured in, casting a warm glow on their workspace.

"Wow, look at all the people!" Bella whispered, her eyes scanning the room.

"Don't worry, Bella. Just focus on our project. We've got this," Max reassured her, giving her a friendly nudge.

With a deep breath, Bella picked up the first block. It was time to bring their vision to life, one block at a time. As she placed it down, the journey of Bella's tower began, a journey that was about to teach her more than she could have ever imagined.

As Bella and Max started building, their table became a canvas of creativity. They worked seamlessly together, Max's practicality perfectly complementing Bella's imaginative designs. The structure they were creating began to take shape – a magnificent tower that seemed to stretch towards the sky, even in its miniature form.

Around them, the community center was alive with the sounds of the contest. Children chattered excitedly, their hands moving deftly as they brought their own visions to life. The hall was a kaleidoscope of colors and shapes, a testament to the boundless creativity of young minds.

"Look at that castle over there, Bella!" Max pointed to a table across the room, where a group of kids was building an elaborate fortress.

Bella glanced over, her eyes wide with admiration. "Wow, that's amazing. But wait till they see our tower!"

As the hours passed, their tower grew taller and more intricate. Bella added a series of small balconies and turrets, her fingers working with precision. Max, meanwhile, focused on reinforcing the base, ensuring that their creation was as sturdy as it was beautiful.

But as they reached the higher levels, Bella realized a problem. The design she had dreamed up was more complex than she had anticipated. The top part of the tower, with its delicate arches and thin walls, was proving to be unstable.

"Max, I think we have an issue," Bella said, her brow furrowed as she tried to add another block to the teetering top.

"What's wrong?" Max asked, looking up from the base.

"The top... it's not as stable as I thought it would be. It's too wobbly," Bella replied, her voice laced with disappointment.

Max stood up and examined the top of the tower closely. "Hmm, you're right. We need to rethink this part."

They both stood in silence for a moment, pondering their next move. The sounds of the contest faded into the background as they focused on the challenge before them.

"Maybe we can simplify the design at the top? Make it less intricate but more stable?" Max suggested.

Bella hesitated. She had envisioned the top of the tower as a grand finale to their creation, a testament to her creativity. But she also knew that without stability, their entire project could come crashing down.

"You might be right, Max. Let's try that," Bella conceded, her voice tinged with a hint of sadness.

Together, they carefully removed the unstable blocks, their fingers working with gentle precision. As they rebuilt the top of the tower, Bella tried to let go of her initial vision and embrace this new, more practical design.

But deep down, she couldn't help but feel a pang of disappointment. Her dream tower, the one she had sketched and imagined so vividly, was evolving into something different, something more realistic but less magical.

As the contest continued, Bella couldn't shake the feeling that her tower, though impressive, wasn't quite the masterpiece she had hoped it would be.

As Bella and Max worked on their revised design, the clock continued to tick, reminding them of the limited time they had left. The tower, now more robust but less ornate, stood tall amongst the creations in the hall. However, Bella couldn't shake off the feeling of disappointment. Her eyes often wandered to the top of the tower, where her dreams had been scaled down to reality.

Max noticed her dismay. "Hey, Bella, it's looking great! Don't be so hard on yourself."

Bella sighed, "It's just not how I imagined it, Max. I wanted it to be... more."

Max pondered for a moment, then his eyes lit up. "Wait, I have an idea. What if we add something unique to the top? Something simple but special?"

Bella's interest was piqued. "Like what?"

"What about a flag? A flag that represents your dream. We could make it colorful and vibrant, just like your imagination," Max suggested enthusiastically.

Bella's face brightened. "That's a brilliant idea, Max! It could be the symbol of our tower!"

They quickly set to work, crafting a small, colorful flag out of some spare materials they found. As Bella placed the flag at the top of the tower, a sense of pride washed over her. It wasn't the intricate design she had initially planned, but it was something unique, something that represented her dreams.

Just as they stepped back to admire their work, a sudden commotion erupted in the hall. A group of kids nearby had accidentally bumped into their own structure, causing it to sway dangerously. The disturbance caused a ripple effect, and before Bella and Max could react, their tower was caught in the chaos.

Time seemed to slow as they watched their tower wobble precariously. Bella's heart sank. All their hard work, all her dreams, were about to come crashing down.

Then, in a moment of quick thinking, Max reached out and steadied the base of the tower. His hands were firm and sure, holding the structure in place against the tremors.

Bella quickly joined in, her hands supporting the middle section. Together, they managed to stabilize the tower, saving it from collapsing.

As the commotion settled and their tower stood firm, Bella and Max looked at each other, a mix of relief and triumph in their eyes.

"We did it, Max! We saved it!" Bella exclaimed, her voice a mixture of surprise and joy.

Max grinned, "We sure did. It's not just about how tall we build, but how well we handle the shakes, right?"

Bella nodded, a newfound understanding dawning on her. The tower was more than just blocks; it was a testament to their teamwork, resilience, and the ability to adapt and overcome challenges.

As the judges began their rounds, Bella looked at their tower, with its colorful flag fluttering proudly at the top. It was a symbol of her dreams, not diminished, but made stronger and more real by the challenges they had overcome.

As the judges made their way around the room, Bella and Max stood by their tower, hands clasped together in anticipation. They watched as the judges admired the other creations, nodding and making notes. Finally, it was their turn. The judges approached Bella's tower, their eyes scanning every detail.

"This is quite a structure," one judge commented, peering at the flag atop the tower.

Bella took a deep breath. "Thank you. It represents my dream."

"And a fine dream it is," another judge smiled. "Very creative and well-executed, especially considering the challenges you faced."

Bella beamed with pride. Max nudged her playfully, whispering, "Told you it was great."

After what felt like an eternity, the judges announced the winners. Bella's heart raced as they called out the names. Third place, second place... but Bella's Tower wasn't mentioned. Disappointment crept in, but before it could take hold, there was a surprise announcement.

"And now, for a special recognition award for creativity and resilience," a judge declared. "This goes to Bella and Max for their extraordinary tower!"

The hall erupted into applause as Bella and Max stepped forward to receive their award. Bella's eyes sparkled, not from winning, but from the realization that her creativity and ability to adapt were just as important as the end result.

As the crowd dispersed, Bella's mother came over, her eyes shining with pride. "You were fantastic, Bella. Your tower is incredible!"

"It didn't win first place, but it's more than I ever hoped for," Bella said, a genuine smile on her face.

Max chimed in, "It's not just about winning. It's about what we learned and how we dealt with the shake-up!"

As they packed up their blocks, Bella looked at the tower one last time. The colorful flag on top caught her eye. It was more than just a piece of cloth; it was a symbol of her journey, her resilience, and her undying creativity.

On their way out, the community center manager approached them. "Bella, that was a fantastic tower. How would you like to display it here for a while? It could inspire other kids."

Bella's eyes widened in surprise and delight. "Really? That would be amazing!"

As they left the community center, Bella felt a sense of accomplishment and growth. She had started the day hoping to build the perfect tower but ended it with something much more valuable: the understanding that creativity is not just about building things up but also about handling the shakes and staying true to your vision.

Bella's tower stood in the community center, a testament to her creativity and resilience. And every time she passed by, she remembered the day she learned that the true foundation of success is not just in the building blocks, but in the lessons learned along the way.

Fiona gazed up at the endless blue sky, her eyes sparkling with wonder as the distant hum of airplane engines filled the air. The local airfield, a canvas of green and grey, bustled with activity. Small planes glided gracefully on the runway, while others soared into the sky, chasing the horizon.

Her family had brought her here for a leisurely weekend outing, but for Fiona, it felt like stepping into a dream. Everywhere she looked, there were aircraft of all shapes and sizes, their wings glinting in the sunlight.

"Look, Mum, that one's about to take off!" Fiona pointed excitedly as a small propeller plane picked up speed on the runway.

Her mother smiled, "It's incredible, isn't it? To think that humans can fly like birds."

As the plane lifted into the air, Fiona's imagination took flight. She pictured herself in the cockpit, navigating through clouds, exploring the vast sky. It was a thrilling thought.

While wandering near the hangars, they met Captain Rivera, a kind-faced pilot with a gentle smile and eyes that seemed to hold countless stories of the sky. He was tinkering with a small, vintage aircraft, his hands skilled and sure.

"Hello there!" he greeted warmly. "Admiring the planes, are we?"

"Yes!" Fiona replied, her voice bubbling with enthusiasm. "I love them! One day, I'm going to fly one myself!"

Captain Rivera chuckled, "Ah, a future pilot! Would you like to learn more about these magnificent machines?"

Fiona nodded eagerly, and the captain began showing her around. He explained how each part of the airplane worked, from the roaring engines to the delicate flaps on the wings.

As they walked, they talked about everything aviation. Fiona listened, fascinated, as Captain Rivera shared tales of his flights, from serene journeys above the clouds to thrilling navigations through storms.

"You know, we have a junior aviation workshop here at the club," Captain Rivera mentioned casually. "It's a place for young enthusiasts like you to learn more about flying."

Fiona's eyes lit up. "Really? Can I join?"

"Of course!" he replied. "It's the perfect place for you to start your journey into the world of aviation."

The idea of actually learning to fly, of understanding the mysteries of the skies, filled Fiona with a thrilling mix of excitement and nervousness. It was an opportunity to step closer to her dream, to soar beyond the clouds.

As they parted ways, Captain Rivera handed her a small brochure about the workshop. "Think about it," he said, "and if you're interested, we'd be delighted to have you."

Fiona clutched the brochure tightly, her heart racing. This was more than just a chance visit to an airfield. It was the beginning of an adventure, a path to the sky, and maybe, just maybe, to her dreams.

That evening, Fiona couldn't stop thinking about the aviation workshop. The stories of Captain Rivera echoed in her mind, each tale a whisper of the adventures that awaited in the skies. She read the brochure over and over, absorbing every detail, every word.

The following Saturday, with the brochure clutched in her hand and her heart pounding with excitement, Fiona arrived at the airfield for her first day at the workshop. The air buzzed with the energy of eager young minds, all gathered with a shared dream of flight.

Captain Rivera greeted her with his warm, reassuring smile. "Welcome, Fiona! Ready to embark on your journey?"

Fiona nodded, her eyes wide with anticipation. The workshop began with a tour of the hangars, where various aircraft rested like sleeping giants. Captain Rivera explained the different types of airplanes, from small single-engine crafts to larger, more complex models.

As they moved from one aircraft to another, Fiona's fascination grew. She learned about the principles of aerodynamics, how the shape of the wings helped lift the plane, and how pilots controlled the aircraft in the air.

"The key to flying is understanding how all these elements work together," Captain Rivera explained. "It's like a dance between the plane and the air around it."

Fiona listened intently, absorbing every word. They then proceeded to a classroom where a small group of other children waited. Here, they delved deeper into the theory of flight, discussing wind currents, weather patterns, and navigation.

After the theory session, Captain Rivera announced, "Now, let's put some of this knowledge into practice. We're going to build model planes and see the principles of aerodynamics in action!"

The children gathered around tables laden with materials – balsa wood, glue, and paint. Fiona worked meticulously on her model, trying to replicate the planes she had seen in the hangars. Captain Rivera moved between the tables, offering guidance and encouragement.

As her model took shape, Fiona felt a surge of pride. It was a tangible representation of her dream, a small step towards her goal of flying.

The day concluded with a flight simulation exercise. One by one, the children took turns in a simulator, a mock cockpit with screens showing virtual skies. Fiona watched as her peers navigated through the simulation, some handling the controls with ease, others finding it more challenging.

When her turn came, Fiona took a deep breath and stepped into the simulator. The cockpit felt surprisingly real, with dials, gauges, and a control stick. Captain Rivera's voice came through the headphones, "Remember, Fiona, flying is about balance and understanding. Take your time and trust what you've learned."

As the simulation began, Fiona felt a mix of nervousness and excitement. She gripped the controls, her fingers trembling slightly. The virtual landscape rolled out before her – a vast expanse of sky and land. She steadied herself, remembering Captain Rivera's words, and gently pushed the throttle.

The simulator responded, and Fiona felt a rush of exhilaration as the virtual plane began to move. She navigated carefully, trying to keep the plane steady. It was harder than she had imagined, the plane swaying and dipping with every movement.

Despite her best efforts, the simulator beeped a warning – she was losing altitude too quickly. Fiona's heart raced as she tried to correct her course, but it was too late. The screen flashed red, signaling a crash.

Fiona stepped out of the simulator, her face flushed with disappointment. Captain Rivera put a reassuring hand on her shoulder. "It's all part of the learning process, Fiona. Every pilot has their share of challenges. What matters is how you overcome them."

As the sun set on the airfield, Fiona watched the planes in the sky, their graceful arcs a reminder of the journey ahead. Today was just the beginning, and she was ready to face whatever challenges lay ahead in her quest to soar.

Weeks passed, and Fiona dedicated herself to learning every aspect of flying. She spent hours at the workshop, practicing on the simulator, building models, and absorbing knowledge from Captain Rivera and the other instructors. Each failure in the simulator became a lesson, each success a step closer to her dream.

Then came the day that would test everything she had learned. Captain Rivera announced a tandem flight – a real flight where Fiona would assist in navigating a small aircraft. Her heart leapt with a mix of excitement and nervousness.

"You've come a long way, Fiona," Captain Rivera said as they walked towards a small, vibrant blue airplane. "Today, you'll get a taste of the real thing. Remember, trust your training and stay calm."

Climbing into the cockpit, Fiona felt a surge of surreal excitement. The dials and controls, once just part of a simulation, were now real and within reach. As the engine roared to life, she felt the plane vibrate with energy.

Captain Rivera guided the takeoff, the ground falling away as they ascended into the sky. Fiona watched in awe, the world below transforming into a patchwork of colors and shapes. She had dreamt of this moment, and now it was real.

"Now, Fiona, let's see what you've learned," Captain Rivera said, handing control of the plane over to her.

Fiona's hands trembled slightly as she took the controls. She focused on keeping the plane level, recalling the techniques she had practiced. The plane responded to her touch, gliding through the air.

"You're doing great," Captain Rivera encouraged. "Remember, flying is about feeling and responding to the plane and the air."

As they flew, dark clouds gathered on the horizon, a sudden storm brewing. Captain Rivera's voice was calm but firm, "Fiona, we need to navigate through this. Remember the techniques for flying in turbulent weather."

Fiona's heart raced as the plane entered the clouds. Rain lashed against the windshield, and the aircraft shook with the force of the wind. She gripped the controls, her knuckles white.

"Steady, Fiona. Adjust the throttle, keep the nose up," Captain Rivera guided.

Fiona focused, her fear transforming into determination. She adjusted the controls, working with the plane and the turbulent air. The storm was a challenge, but she was no longer the timid girl in the simulator. She was a pilot, in control and capable.

Slowly, they emerged from the clouds, the storm behind them. The sky opened up, a vast expanse of calm blue. Fiona let out a breath she didn't know she was holding.

"You did it, Fiona. You navigated through the storm," Captain Rivera's voice was full of pride.

As they headed back to the airfield, Fiona felt a profound sense of achievement. She had faced her fears, trusted her training, and soared beyond the challenge. The sky was not just a dream now; it was a reality she had embraced and conquered.

The plane touched down gently on the runway, the journey through the skies complete. Fiona and Captain Rivera disembarked, their faces lit up with smiles. Fiona felt a sense of triumph that words couldn't capture. She had flown, truly flown, and it was more exhilarating than she had ever imagined.

As they walked back to the clubhouse, Captain Rivera spoke, "Fiona, you handled that brilliantly. You've shown not just skill, but real courage and determination. I'm proud of you."

Fiona beamed with pride. "Thank you, Captain Rivera. I couldn't have done it without your guidance."

Back at the clubhouse, news of Fiona's successful navigation through the storm had spread. The other members of the workshop and club staff gathered around, clapping and cheering for her. She blushed at the attention, feeling a warm sense of belonging.

The club president stepped forward, a kind lady with a beaming smile. "Fiona, your performance today was outstanding. It's my pleasure to present you with the Junior Aviator Badge, a recognition of your hard work, bravery, and skill."

Fiona accepted the badge, her hands trembling with excitement. She pinned it to her jacket, feeling its weight as a symbol of her journey and achievement.

Captain Rivera addressed the gathering. "Fiona's flight today is a testament to what we all believe here at the club: that the sky is just the beginning. With courage and perseverance, there are no limits to what we can achieve."

Fiona looked around at the smiling faces, feeling a deep sense of gratitude and accomplishment. She had started as a dreamer, gazing at planes and yearning for the sky. Now, she was a part of this world, a world where dreams took flight and became reality.

As the celebration continued, Fiona stepped outside, looking up at the sky. The storm clouds had cleared, revealing a vast canvas of blue. She thought about her journey, the challenges, and the lessons learned.

She realized that flying was more than just controlling a plane; it was about facing fears, embracing challenges, and pushing beyond limits. The sky wasn't just a space above the earth; it was a metaphor for life's possibilities.

Fiona knew this was just the beginning. There would be more challenges, more learning, and more adventures. But she was ready for them. With her Junior Aviator Badge shining on her jacket, she felt like she could soar beyond any horizon, reach any height.

As the sun set, casting a golden glow over the airfield, Fiona's heart soared with dreams and possibilities. The sky was only the beginning, and she was ready to fly beyond her wildest dreams.

Leah zipped up her bright blue lab coat and glanced around the bustling school science lab. Beakers bubbled, plants reached towards the light, and every surface was covered with the tools of young scientists at work. Her eyes sparkled with excitement as she turned to her science partner, Ethan.

"Can you believe it's almost time for the science fair, Ethan?" she asked, her voice brimming with anticipation.

Ethan, meticulously organizing their workspace, nodded without looking up. "I know, Leah. We need a plan, something really innovative to stand out."

Just then, Mr. Bentley, their science teacher, clapped his hands for attention. "Class, this year's science fair has a special challenge - the most innovative project will win a special award!"

The room buzzed with excitement. Leah's mind raced with possibilities, while Ethan started jotting down potential ideas in his neat, orderly handwriting.

After class, as they were packing up, Leah noticed a small plant in the corner of the lab, its leaves drooping in the dim light. An idea struck her.

"Ethan, what if we study how different light affects plant growth?" she suggested eagerly.

Ethan looked up, intrigued. "That could work. We could test various light sources – LED, fluorescent, natural light..."

Leah's eyes lit up. "And even colored lights! It could show us something unexpected!"

The next day, they set up a small greenhouse area in the lab. Various plants were carefully labelled and placed under different light sources. Leah bounced around the setup, her enthusiasm infectious.

Ethan, more focused, methodically checked the light intensities and made notes. "We need to be precise with our measurements," he reminded her.

"I know, I know," Leah replied, "but it's just so exciting to think about what we might discover!"

As they worked, their classmates came over to see what they were doing. "What's this for?" asked one of the students, peering at the colorful lights.

"It's our science fair project," Leah explained. "We're testing how different lights affect plant growth. We want to see if we can find a new way to help plants grow better."

Ethan added, "It's all about experimenting and finding out new things. That's what science is all about."

Mr. Bentley walked by and gave them an approving nod. "I like where this is going, Leah and Ethan. Keep up the good work!"

As the bell rang, signaling the end of the day, Leah looked at their setup with pride. "This is going to be great, Ethan. I can feel it!"

Ethan smiled, his usual reserve giving way to a shared sense of excitement. "Yeah, it is. Let's make it the best project we've ever done."

Together, they turned off the lights and left the lab, their minds buzzing with the possibilities that lay ahead.

Over the next few weeks, Leah and Ethan were a whirlwind of activity in the science lab. Each day after school, they rushed to check on their plants, observing changes and recording data with growing excitement.

"Look, Ethan!" Leah exclaimed one afternoon, pointing to a plant under the blue light. "This one's grown taller than the others!"

Ethan peered at the plant, measuring its height. "You're right. The blue light seems to be making a difference. But why?"

They spent hours discussing theories, with Leah suggesting wild, imaginative ideas and Ethan grounding them in scientific principles. Their classmates often stopped by, drawn in by their enthusiasm and the vibrant setup.

One day, as they were examining a plant under the red light, Leah frowned. "This one isn't doing as well. Do you think the red light's too strong?"

Ethan adjusted his glasses, looking concerned. "Maybe. Or it could be something else. We need to investigate further."

They tweaked their experiment, adjusting light intensities and moving plants around to test different conditions. The science fair was approaching, and the pressure was on to make their project stand out.

As they worked, Mr. Bentley often came over to offer guidance and encouragement. "You're doing great work, you two. Remember, science is all about asking questions and finding answers."

One afternoon, they faced an unexpected challenge. A group of younger students, curious about the colorful lights, accidentally knocked over one of the light stands, causing chaos in their carefully arranged setup.

"Oh no, our plants!" Leah cried out, rushing to assess the damage.

Ethan quickly joined her, helping to upright the fallen stand and check on the plants. "It's okay, Leah. We can fix this."

They spent the rest of the afternoon repairing the setup, a sense of determination replacing their initial dismay. Together, they managed to get everything back in order, although some plants looked a bit worse for wear.

"This is just a setback," Ethan said reassuringly. "We'll just have to work a bit harder."

Leah nodded, her resolve strengthened. "We can do this. We'll make our project even better."

In the following days, they noticed some unusual results. A few plants were thriving, while others were lagging behind. Leah and Ethan pondered over these inconsistencies, trying to make sense of them.

One day, Leah had a sudden thought. "What if it's not just about the light? What if there are other factors we're not considering?"

Ethan looked at her, a spark of curiosity in his eyes. "Like what?"

"I'm not sure," Leah admitted. "But let's think outside the box. Let's look at everything - the soil, the water, the temperature."

Energized by this new line of thinking, they expanded their experiment, testing various conditions and eagerly discussing their findings. Each discovery led to more questions, and their project grew in depth and complexity.

As the science fair drew closer, Leah and Ethan worked tirelessly, their partnership a perfect blend of creativity and logic. They were determined to uncover the secrets of their plants' growth, no matter what challenges lay ahead.

With the science fair only a few days away, Leah and Ethan were in the lab every moment they could spare, their experiment becoming more intricate as they delved deeper into their research. The plants under their care had become more than just specimens; they were like silent, green companions on their journey of discovery.

As they arrived one morning, Leah's eyes immediately went to their star plant, a vibrant green specimen that had been thriving under a combination of LED and natural light. But today, something was wrong. The leaves, once perky and bright, were now wilted and drooping.

"Oh no, Ethan, look!" Leah's voice trembled with concern as she pointed at the plant.

Ethan's brow furrowed as he examined it. "This doesn't make sense. It was fine yesterday. What could have changed overnight?"

They checked everything - the light, the water, the soil - but nothing seemed amiss. The clock was ticking, and with their best specimen in trouble, so was their chance at the science fair.

Leah paced back and forth, her mind racing. "We have to figure this out, Ethan. We can't let this ruin our project."

Ethan, usually the calm and collected one, looked equally worried. "Let's go through everything again. There must be something we're missing."

They repeated their tests, going over their notes with a fine-tooth comb. Hours passed, but they were no closer to an answer.

As the lab began to empty, Leah slumped down beside the ailing plant, her spirits as wilted as its leaves. "I thought we had it, Ethan. I thought we were on to something big."

Ethan sat down beside her, trying to muster a reassuring smile. "We were, Leah. We still are. We just need to think... Wait a minute."

He stood up abruptly, his eyes wide with realization. "The temperature, Leah! We've been so focused on light and water that we forgot about the temperature!"

Leah's head snapped up. "The temperature?"

"Yes! Remember how warm it was yesterday? And then the air conditioning was on full blast all night. The sudden change must have shocked it."

Leah jumped to her feet, her energy renewed. "That's it, Ethan! We need to test the temperature effects too!"

They worked feverishly, adjusting the temperature around their plants and carefully monitoring the results. Slowly but surely, the wilted plant began to perk up, its leaves uncurling and reaching towards the light once more.

Leah and Ethan exchanged a look of triumph. "We did it," Leah said, a broad grin spreading across her face.

"We really did," Ethan agreed, his relief palpable.

Their project was back on track, more comprehensive and exciting than ever. They had faced a seemingly insurmountable challenge and had come out stronger for it. As they left the lab that evening, their steps were light with the satisfaction of a problem solved and a lesson learned. The science fair awaited, and they were ready.

The day of the science fair dawned bright and clear, a perfect backdrop for the excitement brewing in the school's gymnasium. Tables lined the room, each showcasing the innovative projects of Leah and Ethan's classmates. But at their table, a crowd had gathered, drawn by the vibrant greenery bathed in different lights and the detailed charts displaying their findings.

Leah beamed as she explained their project to the curious onlookers. "We discovered that not only light but also temperature affects plant growth. See, this plant almost didn't make it, but we figured out that a sudden temperature change was the problem."

Ethan, standing beside her, added, "It was a real challenge, but it taught us the importance of considering all variables in an experiment."

Their science teacher, Mr. Bentley, approached with a smile. "I must say, Leah and Ethan, your project is quite the hit. You've applied scientific principles brilliantly."

As the day progressed, the judges made their rounds, listening intently as Leah and Ethan enthusiastically shared their experiences and findings. Their eyes shone with the thrill of exploration and discovery, their words a testament to their journey.

Finally, the time came for the announcement of the winners. The gymnasium hushed in anticipation as the head judge took the stage. "This year's science fair showcased remarkable talent, but one project stood out for its innovation and comprehensive approach."

Leah gripped Ethan's hand tightly, her heart racing. Ethan gave her an encouraging nod, his own nerves evident.

"And the award for the most innovative project goes to... Leah and Ethan for their study on the effects of light and temperature on plant growth!"

The gymnasium erupted into applause as they made their way to the stage. Their smiles were wide, their steps light with the joy of recognition.

Holding the award, Leah looked out at the sea of faces. "This project taught us so much more than just about plants. We learned that to really discover something, you have to be curious, willing to experiment, and never give up, even when things don't go as planned."

Ethan added, "And it's about teamwork. We couldn't have done this without working together, combining our ideas and efforts."

As the crowd dispersed, Leah and Ethan packed up their project, the award a shiny symbol of their success. But it was the journey that stayed with them - the challenges they overcame, the knowledge they gained, and the partnership they had strengthened.

As they left the gymnasium, Leah turned to Ethan with a mischievous glint in her eye. "So, what should we explore next?"

Ethan laughed, the sound echoing down the hallway. "Whatever it is, I'm in. Let's keep discovering!"

Together, they stepped out into the sunlight, their minds already racing with new ideas and possibilities. The world was a playground of questions, and they were more than ready to explore.

Sarina sat in her favorite corner at home, surrounded by a sea of colorful notebooks and pens. The afternoon sun filtered through the window, casting a warm glow on her latest creation - a story about a magical world hidden in a secret garden. She bit her lip, pondering the next twist in her tale.

Her little writing nook was a kaleidoscope of imagination. Posters of fantastical landscapes adorned the walls, and her bookshelf overflowed with stories of adventure and mystery. This was where Sarina felt most alive, her mind dancing with characters and plots.

At school the next day, the air buzzed with excitement. Mrs. Heynon, Sarina's English teacher, stood at the front of the brightly decorated classroom, her eyes twinkling with an idea.

"Class, this month we're going to embark on a creative journey!" Mrs. Heynon announced, her voice echoing with enthusiasm. "Each of you will write your own story. It can be about anything you like – the only limit is your imagination!"

The class erupted in a chorus of chatter and ideas. Sarina's heart raced. She had countless stories scribbled in her notebooks, but the thought of sharing them made her stomach twist.

As they left the classroom, Sarina's friend Mina bubbled with excitement. "I'm going to write about space pirates!" she exclaimed. Sarina smiled but said nothing, her mind whirling with the possibilities and fears of sharing her own story.

At home that evening, Sarina's parents noticed her pensive mood at dinner. "Everything alright, Sarina?" her dad asked, passing her the bowl of steaming dal.

Sarina nodded, her voice barely above a whisper. "We have to write a story for school. I don't know if mine will be any good."

Her mum smiled warmly. "Sarina, your stories are wonderful. You have a gift."

But Sarina wasn't convinced. That night, as she lay in bed, the shadows of doubt crept into her mind. She thought about her classmates, their ideas so bold and bright. Could her stories really compare?

The next day in class, Mrs. Heynon noticed Sarina's hesitation. "Sarina, you always have such thoughtful ideas in our discussions. I can't wait to read your story," she encouraged.

Sarina felt a flutter of hope in her chest. Maybe she could share her secret garden story. It was full of magic and mystery, just the way she liked it. Taking a deep breath, Sarina decided she would try. She would write her story, not just for the assignment, but for herself.

That evening, Sarina opened her notebook and began to write. The words flowed like a river, each one a stepping stone into the magical world she had created. For the first time, she felt ready to share a piece of her world.

Over the next few days, Sarina's notebook became her closest companion. She scribbled during recess, under the old oak tree in the schoolyard, her pen racing across the pages. The story about the secret garden grew, blooming with mysterious characters and hidden paths.

In class, Mrs. Heynon would sometimes peer over her shoulder, offering words of encouragement. "Your story seems to be coming along wonderfully, Sarina," she'd say with a smile. Sarina would blush, nodding shyly, the warm feeling of pride bubbling inside her.

However, not all moments were filled with such ease. One afternoon, while Sarina was deeply engrossed in her writing, her classmate Jake peeked over her shoulder. "What are you writing, Sarina? A fairy tale?" he teased, his voice loud enough for others to hear.

Sarina's cheeks flushed with embarrassment. She quickly shut her notebook, hiding her words from prying eyes. "It's just a story," she mumbled, feeling her confidence waver.

Later, in the playground, Mina approached Sarina, her brow furrowed with concern. "Don't mind Jake," she said. "He's always teasing. But I bet your story is amazing."

Sarina forced a smile, her heart still racing from the incident. "Thanks, Mina. I just... I want it to be good, you know?"

As days turned into weeks, the deadline for the story project drew closer. Sarina poured her heart into every word, her secret garden world becoming more vivid with each line. Yet, the fear of sharing it, of being judged, loomed over her like a dark cloud.

In class, other students began to share snippets of their stories. Dragons, superheroes, and faraway galaxies filled the room with excitement. Sarina listened, her admiration mixed with a growing sense of doubt. Could her story about a magical garden really stand out?

One morning, Mrs. Heynon announced, "Next week, we'll have a special story sharing session. Everyone will get a chance to read a part of their story aloud."

The class buzzed with excitement, but Sarina felt a knot tighten in her stomach. Reading her story aloud? The thought was terrifying.

At home, Sarina's mum noticed her subdued mood. "What's wrong, dear?" she asked gently, sitting beside her at the dinner table.

Sarina sighed, fiddling with her fork. "We have to read our stories out loud in class. I'm scared people won't like mine."

Her mum wrapped an arm around her. "Sarina, every story is special because it comes from the heart. Yours will be wonderful."

But Sarina wasn't so sure. That night, she lay in bed, her mind racing with anxiety. Would her classmates understand her story? Would they laugh, or worse, be bored?

The next few days, Sarina's excitement for her story wavered. She began to question every word, every character. The joy of writing was replaced with fear, and for the first time, her magical garden felt like a distant dream.

The day of the story sharing session arrived. Sarina's hands trembled as she clutched her notebook. Her classmates were buzzing with excitement, each eager to share their tales. Sarina, however, felt like a tiny boat lost in a sea of confident voices.

Mrs. Heynon began the session with encouraging words. "Remember, everyone, this is a celebration of our creativity. There's no right or wrong in storytelling."

One by one, her classmates stood up, their stories bringing to life superheroes, talking animals, and adventures in outer space. Sarina's heart pounded in her chest as her turn approached.

Finally, Mrs. Heynon called her name. "Sarina, would you like to share your story with us?"

Sarina stood up, her legs feeling like jelly. She opened her notebook, her eyes scanning the first lines she had written weeks ago. The room fell silent, all eyes on her.

Taking a deep breath, Sarina began to read. Her voice was shaky at first, but as she delved into the world of her secret garden, her confidence began to grow. She described the vibrant flowers that whispered secrets, the ancient trees that told tales of old, and the mysterious creatures that danced in the moonlight.

The class listened, captivated by the vivid imagery and the enchanting world Sarina had created. As she read, Sarina forgot about her fears, lost in the magic of her own story.

Then, she reached the climax of her tale – the moment the garden's secret was revealed. Her voice rose with excitement, her words painting a picture so vivid it was as if the garden had come to life in the classroom.

As she finished, the room burst into applause. Sarina looked up, her heart swelling with a mix of relief and joy. Her classmates' faces beamed with admiration and awe.

"That was incredible, Sarina!" Mina exclaimed, clapping enthusiastically.

Even Jake, who had teased her before, looked impressed. "I didn't know you could write like that," he admitted.

Mrs. Heynon smiled warmly. "Sarina, your story was beautiful. You have a wonderful talent for making your readers feel as if they are right there in the garden with you."

Sarina felt a weight lift off her shoulders. She had faced her fear, shared her story, and it had resonated with her classmates. The doubt that had clouded her mind faded away, replaced by a newfound sense of pride and accomplishment.

As the session ended, her classmates crowded around, asking questions about her garden and its inhabitants. Sarina answered, her heart full of happiness. She realized then that her voice mattered, that her stories could touch others, and that there was nothing to fear in sharing a piece of her world.

After the story sharing session, Sarina's world transformed. Her classmates, who once knew her as the quiet girl in the corner, now saw her as a brilliant storyteller. She felt a sense of belonging she had never experienced before.

As the days passed, Sarina found herself surrounded by friends during recess, all eager to hear more about her secret garden. Her notebook, once a private sanctuary, became a shared treasure among her peers.

One sunny afternoon, Mrs. Heynon approached Sarina with a twinkle in her eye. "Sarina, I've been thinking," she began, "how would you feel about starting a writing club at school? You could help others find their voice, just like you found yours."

Sarina's eyes widened with excitement. "Really? I would love that!" she exclaimed, the idea igniting a spark within her.

The following week, the writing club had its first meeting. Sarina stood at the front of the room, her heart full of pride as she looked at the eager faces before her. "Welcome to the Storytellers' Club," she announced. "Here, we'll share our stories, our ideas, and most importantly, our voices."

The club became a haven for creativity, with students from all grades coming together to write and share their stories. Sarina felt a deep sense of fulfillment, guiding her peers and encouraging them to express themselves.

One evening, as Sarina sat in her nook at home, her mum peeked in. "You seem different, Sarina. Happier," she observed, her voice soft with affection.

Sarina nodded, her face aglow. "I am, Mum. I've learned that my stories can touch people's hearts. That my voice matters."

Her mum smiled, her eyes reflecting pride. "I always knew they would, my dear."

The school year drew to a close with a special assembly. Mrs. Heynon took the stage, her eyes scanning the audience until they rested on Sarina. "This year, one of our students has shown exceptional talent and bravery in sharing her unique voice. Sarina, please come up here."

Sarina's heart leaped as she walked onto the stage, her classmates applauding loudly. Mrs. Heynon handed her a certificate and whispered, "Your story will also be featured in our school's annual magazine."

Sarina beamed, her eyes scanning the crowd, meeting the faces of her friends, her teachers, and her proud parents. She realized that her journey with her secret garden had taught her more than just the joy of storytelling. It had taught her the power of self-expression, the importance of being true to oneself, and the magic that happens when one shares their unique perspective with the world.

As she stepped off the stage, Sarina knew this was just the beginning. Her stories, her voice, would continue to grow, just like the magical garden in her notebook. And she couldn't wait to see where they would take her next.

CONCLUSION

As we turn the last page of "Stories of Discovery: Leadership for Girls," our hope is that these narratives have kindled a flame of ambition, creativity, and resilience within you.

Remember, every remarkable achiever, much like the heroines in these stories, began with a dream and the determination to make it a reality.

Take these tales along as you set forth on your own path, and may your adventure be as empowering and transformative as those of the extraordinary young girls you've journeyed with in these pages.

Made in the USA
Las Vegas, NV
03 October 2024

96227014R00049